Bright ≡Summaries.com

The Bourgeois gentilhomme

by Molière

BOOK ANALYSIS

Written by Vincent Jooris
Translated by Oliver Brown

The Bourgeois gentilhomme

BY MOLIÈRE

MOLIERE

FRENCH PLAYWRIGHT, ACTOR AND THEATRE DIRECTOR

- **Born in 1622 in Paris**

- **Died in 1673 in the same town**

- **Some of his works:**

    - *Dom Juan* (1665), comedy

    - *The Miser* (1668), comedy

    - *Le Malade imaginaire* (1673), comedy-ballet

Molière (whose real name was Jean-Baptiste Poquelin) was born in Paris into the wealthy bourgeoisie. He turned to the theatre at an early age and founded the Illustre-Théâtre company (1643-1645) with the actress Madeleine Béjart (1618-1672). After 13 years of itinerant theatre in the provinces, he returned to Paris, where he was noticed by King Louis XIV (1638-1715), who took him into his service and placed him under his protection.

Molière mainly wrote comedies in which, under the guise of laughter, he exposed the faults of his contemporaries (preciosity, pedantry, avarice, etc.) and criticised certain members of 17th-century society (authoritarian fathers, false devotees, charlatan doctors, etc.)

On 17 February 1673, he fell ill on stage during a performance of Le *Malade imaginaire* and died at home that evening. His many plays still have a considerable influence today and make him a major author of the classical century.

THE BOURGEOIS GENTILHOMME

MR. JOURDAIN OR THE FOLLY OF GRANDEUR

- **Genre:** comedy-ballet

- **Reference edition:** *Le Bourgeois gentilhomme, Le Médecin malgré lui*, Paris, Maxi-Livres, 2005, 158 p.

- **1st edition:** 1670

- **Themes:** bourgeoisie, arrivisme, ridicule, parvenus, social climbing, education

First performed in 1670 at the court of Louis XIV, *Le Bourgeois gentilhomme is* a comedy-ballet by Molière, which combines the music of Jean-Baptiste Lully (French composer of Italian origin, 1632-1687) with dance interludes by Pierre Beauchamp (French dancer and ballet master, 1631-1705).

A very rich bourgeois, Mr. Jourdain is a parvenu. Seized by the folly of grandeur, he wishes to join the aristocracy. He tries to learn the manners of the aristocracy (thanks to private lessons given to him by masters), courts a marquise and seeks a noble son-in-law. But he only succeeds in being mocked and swindled by everyone.

This famous play, the forerunner of the musical, has been performed thousands of times since its creation, making it a classic. It has also been adapted several times for film and opera.

ACT I

Scene I

The music master and the dancing master are pleased to have Mr. Jourdain as a pupil, because, although he has little knowledge of the nobility, he pays them well. In addition to the money, the dancing master appreciates the praise he receives for practising his art, as it flatters his ego.

Scene II

Mr. Jourdain arrives. The two masters hypocritically admire his attire and pay him many compliments – even though their guest is in fact dressed only in a dressing gown and a bonnet.

Mr. Jourdain then listens to a serenade composed by the music master's disciple, which he finds gloomy. He then sang a light ditty; both masters complimented him, and each assured him of the indispensability of his art.

The scene ends with a musical interlude composed of three musicians, which pleases Mr. Jourdain very much.

ACT II

Scene I

Mr. Jourdain proves the crudeness of his artistic tastes by confessing to liking the marine trumpet, an instrument known to make an unmelodious noise. He agrees to a music concert at his home once a week, as the music master says this is a custom observed by people of quality.

Mr. Jourdain then announces the arrival of the Marquise Dorimène that very evening. He then wants to learn to curtsy.

Scenes II and III

The master of arms arrives, and Mr. Jourdain demonstrates his clumsiness (by not being able to defend himself against a simple foil attack) and utters nonsense (by understanding that a man, if he knows how to make the right wrist movements when handling the foil, is sure not to be killed by his opponent).

When the master of arms asserts the superiority of his art, an argument breaks out between the three teachers. Mr. Jourdain tries to intervene, but no one pays him any attention.

The philosophy teacher then appears and asserts that it is philosophy that dominates all disciplines. The fight resumes and Mr. Jourdain, tired of being ignored, lets them fight amongst themselves.

Scene IV

When the argument is over, the philosophy teacher begins his lecture with a Latin quotation (*"Nam sine doctrina vita est quasi mortis imago"*: without science, life is an image of death), which the bourgeois pretends to understand in order to appear educated. The teacher then asks him what he wants to learn. Mr. Jourdain refuses to discuss logic, morals and physics, which he considers boring and uninteresting; he thus proves that he has not understood his interlocutor's Latin phrase at all.

Mr. Jourdain prefers to learn spelling. The teacher of philosophy decides to give him a lesson on vowels and their pronunciation – which is quite far from his favourite field. His host repeats the vowels with candour and ridicule.

At the end of the lesson, the bourgeois asks the teacher to help him write some words to seduce the marquise. At this point, he shows a new facet of his ignorance: he does not know what prose is. He insists that the master of philosophy write something similar to "beautiful marquise, your beautiful eyes make me die of love": he has not yet written the note intended for Dorimène and would like the master to modify it to make it as forceful as possible. The latter suggests alternatives, before admitting that the wording initially used by Mr. Jourdain is the best. Jourdain boasts that he found this formula, thanks to his natural talent.

Scene V

The master tailor comes to deliver his order. Mr. Jourdain complains that his stockings are hurting him and, when presented with a garment on which the flowers are shown upside down, he expresses his astonishment. The tailor makes up for his mistake by assuring him that this is how people of quality wear flowers, which is a blatant lie to keep in the good graces of the bourgeois. Mr. Jourdain immediately agrees to wear the garment.

The tailor boys, the master's assistants, use noble terms to address Mr. Jourdain ("gentleman", "your highness"), which flatters him. To reward them, the bourgeois gives them money.

ACT III

Scenes I to III

Mr. Jourdain goes for a walk to show off his new clothes. Nicole, the maid, laughs at his ridiculous attire. Mr. Jourdain tells her that guests are coming that evening, which interrupts her laughter and puts her in a bad mood.

Mrs. Jourdain then arrives and berates her husband about his dreams of nobility; she assures him that many people make fun of him and his behaviour. Nicole complains about the extra work involved in the parade of masters. Vexed, Mr. Jourdain blames their ignorance and tries to demonstrate his knowledge by referring to his pronunciation lesson.

Mrs. Jourdain also deplores the fact that a lord, Dorante, keeps borrowing money from them. Unlike her husband, she does not believe that he will ever pay them back.

Scenes IV and V

Dorante arrives and immediately flatters Mr. Jourdain. He promises to pay off his debts and manages to get even more money: Mr. Jourdain is once again fooled, for he can refuse nothing to a man who speaks of him to the king and covers him with compliments.

Dorante is looking for Lucile, Mr. Jourdains' daughter because he wants to see her. Mrs. Jourdain, who is not fooled by his hypocritical flattery, humorously taunts him.

Scene VI

Dorante confirms the arrival of the Marquise Dorimène: he plays matchmaker. He insists that women like to be showered with gifts. Mr. Jourdain, who hopes to seduce the Marquise, makes sure that his wife is not present for dinner; he wants to avoid any embarrassment. Nicole spies on the conversation on behalf of Mrs. Jourdain, but the two men leave the scene as soon as they spot her.

Scene VII

Nicole reports to Mrs. Jourdain. She is not surprised by her husband's flightiness and does not take it personally. She would especially like her daughter to marry Cléonte, her suitor. She, therefore, orders Nicole to send for him to ask for Lucile's hand.

Scenes VIII to X

Nicole reaches Cleonte. He and his valet, Covielle, do not want to hear anything she has to say; they promptly chase her away. In fact, both men complain that they have previously been ignored in a chance encounter Cléonte by Lucile, and Covielle by Nicole, whose lover he is. Nevertheless, Cléonte remains in love with Lucile, and Covielle is equally in love with Nicole.

The latter then tells Lucile about the bad reception she received at Cléonte's house. The young women try to clear up the misunderstanding, and their suitors finally listen to their explanations. They were accompanied by an old aunt for whom the mere approach of a man dishonours a young girl. The two couples are reconciled.

Scenes XI to XV

Cléonte asks Lucile to marry him, but Mr. Jourdain rejects the young man's proposal because he is not a 'gentleman'. Cléonte is, however, on the same level as the Jourdain family on the social ladder.

An argument ensues between Mr. and Mrs. Jourdain about the family's interests: Mrs. Jourdain would like her daughter to marry a man of the same social rank; Mr. Jourdain, on the other hand, would like to make his daughter a marquise.

Cléonte is desperate, but Covielle has a plan to convince Mr. Jourdain: they retire to discuss it, while Mr. Jourdain, left alone, regrets not being born a nobleman.

Scenes XVI to XX

Dorante and Dorimène are announced. As they talk, we understand that Dorante is passing off Mr. Jourdain's gifts as his own and that he wants to marry the Marquise. The latter is impressed by his gifts to woo her, but she is unaware that Dorante is living on loans and manipulating her.

Mr. Jourdain interrupts them. Dorante discreetly advises him not to talk about the diamond he has given her, to avoid his deception being discovered. The act ends with the arrival of the lackey, who invites the protagonists to the table.

ACT IV

Scene I

The dinner is set to music. Dorante takes credit for this with Dorimène. Mr. Jourdain is thoughtful, despite his usual awkwardness. At the table, Dorante carefully avoids the subject of the diamond, but Dorimène realises Mr. Jourdain's gallantry, which irritates Dorante.

Scenes II to IV

Mrs. Jourdain catches her husband flattering Dorimène. When Dorante claims to be the one who ordered the meal, Mr. Jourdain, too naive and under the Count's control, thinks he is covering for him. But it is only a matter of protecting his interests with the Marquise.

Mrs. Jourdain is not fooled and calls everyone out. Dorimène, who does not understand the situation, leaves the room in a huff. Dorante accompanies her home. Mr. Jourdain demands an apology from his wife; in vain. She leaves him alone and angry.

Scenes V to VIII

Covielle enters disguised as a Turk. He introduces himself as a friend of Mr. Jourdain's father: to gain his trust, he makes him believe that his father was a noble gentleman, not a merchant. He then announces that the son of the Grand Turk wishes to marry Lucile. But for this union to take place, Mr. Jourdain must be made a "mamamouchi" – an honorary title invented by Molière – a Turkish nobleman.

Obviously, he accepts. Cléonte then arrives, also disguised as a Turk. Covielle serves as interpreter. The ennoblement ceremony is a musical interlude and involves beating with sticks and swords. Dorante is informed of the deception by Covielle, who laughs at his ingenuity.

ACT V

Scenes I to III

Mrs. Jourdain asks her husband to explain his Turkish disguise. He gets angry and speaks Turkish. His wife thinks he is mad. Dorante supports Cléonte's masquerade and takes advantage of it to persuade Dorimène to get married: she no longer wants him to spend money courting her. The Count also congratulates Mr. Jourdain, who apologises for his wife's behaviour and sends for his daughter to marry the Turk.

Scenes IV to VI

Mr. Jourdain introduces Lucile to her future husband. At first, she refuses to marry him, but when she recognises Cléonte, she finally accepts. She passes off this change of heart as a sudden desire to please her father – which delights him.

Scene VII

Mrs. Jourdain is strongly opposed to the marriage, but when Covielle informs her of the deception (by taking her aside to reveal his plan, without Mr. Jourdain hearing it), she finally agrees.

Dorante also announces his marriage to Dorimène, which appeases Mrs. Jourdain's jealousy. Mr. Jourdain thinks it is a trick and lets it happen, still hoping to marry the

Marquise. He also gives Nicole's hand to Covie le. A triple wedding is thus planned.

While waiting for the notary, everyone is entertained by the show given in honour of the guests: the *Ballet of the Nations* (Spanish, Italian and French). This part alone lasts as long as the comedy.

CHARACTER STUDY

MR. JOURDAIN

A wealthy cloth merchant, Mr. Jourdain has virtually no education. He dreams of being like the nobles, but he does not know their ways. He, therefore, spends lavishly to learn their ways and customs, to make connections and to approach the court. His main goal is to seduce the Marquise Dorimène in order to rise socially.

Extremely gullible, he is soon spotted by swindlers who extort a lot of money from him. At once naive, vain and clumsy, Mr. Jourdain sometimes elicits laughter – at his own expense – and sometimes pity. For example, when he greets the various instructions of his teachers with a series of "uh?" that shows his total lack of understanding.

However, Mr. Jourdain is not ingenuous. In order to carry out his plot, he is suspicious of everyone, because he knows he is being watched. And in fact, he is the object of everyone's gaze – that of his exploiters, his servants, his wife, etc. – often malicious, mocking or reproving.

The character of the spoilt child is omnipresent and sustains the whole play. Molière himself played this role, which has since become a success for other actors in the centuries that followed.

MRS. JOURDAIN

Mr. Jourdain's wife does not deny her bourgeois status. She embodies good sense and order in the face of her husband's eccentric madness. The latter's excesses leave her distraught, especially as he excludes her from his plans. She is left with mockery and patience as a last resort. On several occasions, she calls her husband 'mad', which illustrates her powerlessness in the face of the enormity of his aspirations.

Mrs. Jourdain always supports what she believes to be right – for example, she refuses to allow her daughter to marry the Turk (who she does not know is Cléonte) – and also knows how to defend her family's interests when they are threatened. For example, she is suspicious of Dorante, fearing that he will swindle her husband.

Finally, this character provides a useful contrast to the economy and comedy of the play. The more sensible and composed Mrs. Jourdain seems, the more ridiculous and credulous Mr. Jourdain looks:

> *"MADAME JOURDAIN – Yes, he is kind to you, and caresses you, but he borrows your money.*
>
> *MONSIEUR JOURDAIN – Well, isn't it an honour to lend money to a man in that condition? And can I do less for a lord who calls me his dear friend?*
>
> *MADAME JOURDAIN – And what does this lord do for you?*
>
> *MONSIEUR JOURDAIN – Things that one would be surprised at, if one knew them. (act III, scene III)*

DORANTE

Dorante presents himself as a count, but is he really? Doubt hovers throughout the play, but is never removed. Between Mr. Jourdain and the Marquise Dorimène, he serves as an intermediary and matchmaker: he transmits the words – sometimes modifying them – of these two interlocutors who are not speaking directly to each other.

But beyond appearances, his motives are clearly selfish, and he has no regard for Mr. Jourdain, whom he has been swindling for some time. A skilled manipulator and liar, Dorante exploits Mr. Jourdain's aspirations and candour to serve his own interests. He extorts money from him without scruples – pretending to support his rise – and seduces Dorimene in his place, passing off her gifts as his own.

THE MASTERS

At Mr. Jourdain's house, masters come and go at all hours, and all are experts in their respective fields: dance, music, fencing, philosophy and dress. These are the disciplines that one must master when one is a nobleman if one wishes to be seen as such; hence Mr. Jourdain's interest in them.

The masters benefit financially from Mr. Jourdain's obsessions. That is why they are particularly sweet and considerate in his presence. But this is hypocrisy, for in truth, they all despise him. He does not belong to their world, does not understand their codes, has neither the finesse nor the intelligence, nor even the patience that would allow him to practise the various arts they teach:

> *"MUSIC MASTER – [...] He is a man, indeed, whose lights are small, who speaks falsely of all things, and applauds only in the wrong way; but his money straightens the judgments of his mind. He has discernment in his purse. (Act I, scene I)*

Dishonest profiteers, engage in futile arguments with one another in which each asserts the superiority of his discipline, and in which, above all, they show themselves to be at least as foolish as Mr. Jourdain. In the final analysis, the picture they give of the nobility is therefore hardly more flattering than the one given of the bourgeoisie by Mr. Jourdain.

DORIMENE

The Marquise Dorimène is a capricious widow whom Mr. Jourdain tries to seduce in order to take advantage of her title. To this end, he ruins himself with sumptuous gifts, but he also hopes to please her with the nobility of his spirit. Moreover, during the dinner party to which he has invited her, Dorimène seems to show some interest in the bourgeois – which disturbs Dorante.

She is fooled by Mr. Jourdain, but also by Dorante, who makes her believe that all the gifts are from him. However, Dorante's ploy works, as she is about to marry him at the end of the play.

THE YOUNG BOURGEOIS: LUCILE AND CLÉONTE

Lucile is the only child of the Jourdains. She embodies the stereotype of the fragile, amorous and naive young girl. Her mother encourages her to love Cléonte, while her father wants to impose a marriage that serves his own interests.

Cleonte embodies another cliché: that of the young, honest and upright leading man; he is the passionate lover, ready to do anything to seduce his lover.

The couple of lovers who are promised to each other – and who manage to get married at the end of the play – is a recurrent element in the comedies of the classical period.

THE SERVANTS: NICOLE AND COVIELLE

Nicole is Mrs. Jourdain's servant. As a woman of the people, she allows herself to laugh loudly and unabashedly at her master's extravagances. Covielle, Cleonte's valet, is also Nicole's lover. Naturally pragmatic and cunning, it is he who devises a stratagem – the invention of the Grand Turk – to help his master.

Servants are also recurrent in classical plays. Through these characters, Molière gained the sympathy and support of a more popular section of the public.

A COMEDY-BALLET

Without abandoning farces (*Sganarelle ou le Cocu imaginaire* [1660]; *Les Fourberies de Scapin* [1671]), Molière specialised in comedies of manners: he openly caricatured the shortcomings of the society of his time, even if it meant causing controversy (*Les Précieuses ridicules* [1659]; *L'École des femmes* [1662]; *Le Tartuffe ou l'Hypocrite* [1664]; *Dom Juan; Le Misanthrope* [1666]; and *L'Avare* [The Miser]). Before him, comedy was a genre considered largely inferior to tragedy (inspired, at the time, by the authors of Antiquity); it was, thanks to his impressively successful plays that the genre gained its letters of nobility.

But Molière was also, with Jean-Baptiste Lully, the inventor of a new genre: the comédie-ballet, the ancestor of the musical, of which *Le Bourgeois gentilhomme* and *Le Malade imaginaire* are undoubtedly the most representative examples.

The first comedy-ballet was *Les Fâcheux*, in 1661. It was already common practice at the time to place comic interludes in ballets to give the dancers time to change between scenes, but where Molière broke new ground was in establishing a continuity of storyline between the danced and acted passages. In fact, at the time of their creation, the comedies-ballets were set up to be integrated into a ballet: in the case of Le *Bourgeois gentilhomme*, the play was followed by the *Ballet des nations*.

The comedy-ballet uses the same comic devices as the canonical comedy (comedy of gesture, situation, character and words), but adds moments of song and dance. It should not be confused with the opera-ballet: where the latter is more dispersed in the plot, the comedy-ballet follows a single action and does not bother with secondary actions. Its central subject very often revolves around the question of the marriage of contemporary, ordinary characters, representatives of the everyday life of the time.

In 1670, King Louis XIV, always eager for entertainment, commissioned the musician Lully to write a ballet (at the time, a dance and song performance). At first, Molière was only asked to write a few words of the libretto. But Molière did not want to be satisfied with having Turks 'gibber' and valets dance. So he wrote a whole play. The playwright wanted to incorporate dance into the action and strengthen the expression of feelings through music. Nevertheless, the entertainment is almost never juxtaposed with the comedy, but is a natural extension of it. It is therefore a complete show.

During their ten years of collaboration, Molière and Lully (assisted by Pierre Beauchamp) created eight comedy-ballets: *Les Fâcheux*, *L'Amour médecin* (1665), *Pastorale comique* (1667), *Le Sicilien ou l'Amour peintre* (1667), *George Dandin ou le Mari confondu* (1668), *Monsieur de Pourceaugnac* (1669), *Les Amants magnifiques* (1670) and *Le Bourgeois gentilhomme*.

THE FASHION FOR TURQUERIES

The Ottoman Empire (1299-1923) was very influential in the time of Louis XIV and extended as far as Austria. It was also a major trading power: silks, tapestries, spices, sugar cane, cotton and other luxury goods passed through this country. For these reasons, some European monarchies fought the Turks, while others sought to make allies of them. However, by the time Molière wrote *The Bourgeois Gentleman*, the Ottoman Empire was no longer considered a military threat, even though it occupied the Balkans.

In any case, this civilisation aroused the admiration of Westerners: they were truly fascinated by the exoticism of this distant land, still little known in the West. It was in this context that the "Turqueries" appeared, i.e. works of art developed in Western Europe that represented or imitated Turkish culture, for example in the fields of music (the first entry in Jean-Philippe Rameau's [French composer, 1683-1764] opera-ballet, *Les Indes galantes*, is entitled "The Generous Turk") or opera: *The Abduction from the Seraglio*, whose music was developed by Mozart [German composer, 1756-1791]; the *Turkish March*, a sonata by the same Mozart, etc.

Under Louis XIV, the Ottoman Sultan Mehmed IV (1642-1693) had the French ambassador in Istanbul expelled, but wishing to re-establish good relations between the two powers, he sent an emissary to Versailles in November 1669: Soliman Aga. This Turkish emissary dazzled all those who came in his path; the pomp and circumstance he displayed were a testament to the power of the Sultan. But once he arrived at his destination, Suleiman Aga disregarded the sumptuous welcome he received and looked down on the French monarchy. This diplomatic visit left a deep impression. Despite the exoticism that still captivated the court, no one forgot the indignation caused by this event.

In *Le Bourgeois gentilhomme*, Turkish fashion appears through Cléonte's disguise. This directly confers on him the status of a nobleman in the eyes of the admiring Mr. Jourdain, who immediately proposes his daughter in marriage. Was Molière to avenge the insolent coldness of the arrogant emissary who had snubbed the king? In any case, his fairy-tale buffoonery seduced everyone.

A COMICAL PLAY

A buffoonery and a farce

Le Bourgeois gentilhomme can be likened to buffoonery – a theatrical genre with its roots in the Middle Ages – in that the play plays on the ridiculous and grotesque, whether through characters (here, staging the aberrant ambitions of Mr. Jourdain) or through disguises (for example, the costume of a Turk, which the protagonist wears voluntarily in order to be ennobled).

But the play is also part of the farce, a genre of medieval origin, traditionally reserved for the common people (as opposed to comedy, which is aimed at a bourgeois audience, and tragedy, which is aimed at a noble audience), which brings to the stage the laughable intrigues of people of middle and low status, in a style that is often crude and coarse.

Following his travels in Italy, Molière – who became famous in this vein with plays such as *Le Docteur amoureux* (1658) and, later, *Les Fourberies de Scapin* – was inspired by the popular genre of *commedia dell'arte*, its characters and its procedures; he introduced several of them into his theatre: among them, the lazzi (acrobatic movements accompanied by buffoonish wordplay, as in the supposed ennoblement ceremony of Mr. Jourdain), buffoonish humour and the comic device of quiproquo. Through his theatrical work, Molière restored a certain cachet to the genre of farce, which was then considered unworthy of the interest of the bourgeois and the nobility in France.

Four distinct comic springs

Traditionally, comedies generate laughter by relying on four main sources: gestures, characters, situations and words. Unsurprisingly, these are all used by the playwright in *Le Bourgeois gentilhomme* :

- **Comique de geste** is a type of comedy induced by laughable movements (such as the delivery of blows). It is, however, the least present comic in the play. It traditionally appears in didascalies or can be added by the director when adapting for the stage. It appears, for example, in Act II, Scene II: "*The master-at-arms pushes two or three boots at him and says, 'En garde! ' "*) ;

- **Character comedy** is based on the character traits of one or more characters that trigger laughter, either by their ridiculousness or by their multiple appearances in the text. This is probably the most developed form of comedy in the play. The character of Mr. Jourdain (his naivety, vanity, and ambition) is the most blatant and telling example: throughout the text, his desires for greatness are mocked and ridiculed constantly. Scene IV of Act III, where the bourgeois is quick to give money to Dorante – who swindles him – is one of many examples of the mockery of the protagonist;

- **the comique de situation** is found several times in the work: it is a comique where the situation generates laughter by its ridiculous or rocambolical character. For example, the fourth scene of Act II, in which Mr. Jourdain ridiculously repeats vowels, or the few scenes in which the spectator (or the reader) knows that Cleonte is in fact the Turk in disguise. Indeed, one of the privileged manifestations of situational comedy is the quiproquo: the spectator is aware of a particular situation – as may be some of the protagonists – but other characters are unaware of what is really going on. This unequal distribution of knowledge is intended to provoke laughter. Here, this is the case when Cleonte appears, disguised as a Turk (Act IV, scene VI), since the spectator, unlike Mr. Jourdain, has previously been made aware of the deception;

- Finally, there is also **word comedy**. It is manifested in puns, in the use of unusual terms, in the confusion between several similar words, etc. For example, in Act III, Scene V, Mrs. Jourdain replies ironically to Dorante, who asks her how her daughter is doing: "She's doing fine on her two legs. Of course, Mr. Jourdain's use of a supposedly Turkish dialect when he meets Cleonte ("Strouf, strif, strof, straf", Act V, Scene IV) makes the audience laugh.

A SATIRE ON THE UPSTARTS

In many of his plays, Molière dramatises and ridicules – sometimes cynically – the dangers of excess, egoism, hypocrisy and vanity; on the other hand, he always promotes the advantages of reasonable behaviour. Thus, a practical morality generally emerges from his works, and this is still the case here, in *Le Bourgeois gentilhomme*.

Some individuals acquire wealth and success very quickly. They may then feel the need to adorn themselves with luxurious objects, to seek, by all means, to ostensibly show the level of influence and power they have just attained. But often, their origins continue to show behind this new façade and betray the nature of their condition. They are what is commonly known as the 'nouveau riche', the 'parvenus': people who have acquired a higher social status, but who have not managed to adopt the manners of that status.

In the 17TH century, there were wealthy people of commoner extraction, and a minority of them were obsessed with the image they gave in society. These presumptuous bourgeois imitate those they envy and take the

aristocrats as models. The desire to dazzle is sometimes transformed into a folie de grandeur.

Thus, in *Le Bourgeois gentilhomme*, Mr. Jourdain – like
George Dandin, the hero of the play of the same name –
believes that he can become a member of the nobility
by appropriating, through money and education, the
characteristics of this social class: appearance, language, culture and manners. And it is with this in mind
that he summons to his home a host of masters of all
kinds.

However, Mr. Jourdain struggles to adopt the codes of
nobility: he is clumsy during his fencing lesson (Act II,
scene II), he enjoys rude music, unworthy of a nobleman
(Act I, scene II), he demonstrates his lack of culture as
soon as he opens his mouth (Act II, scene IV), etc. He is
also unable to recognise the codes and practices of
nobility, for example by accepting a ridiculous lesson
on vowel pronunciation instead of a physics lesson (Act
II, scene II), which a true nobleman, or at least someone
familiar with the noble world, would never have done.

Mr. Jourdain cultivates his obsession with excess and
pushes it to the point of ridicule. We watch for the
moment when he finally implodes, like the frog that
wants to be as big as the ox in the fable by La Fontaine
(French poet, 1621-1695). And Molière mocks him merci-
lessly because he thinks he is different and tries to rise
above his rank. No doubt he shares the opinion
expressed by Cleonte in this long tirade:

> *"CLÉONTE – [...] I think that any imposture is unworthy of an honest man, and that there is cowardice in disguising what heaven has given us, in adorning ourselves in the eyes of the world with a stolen title, in wanting to give ourselves for what we are not. I was born of parents, no doubt, who held honourable offices. I have acquired the honour of six years' service in the army, and I have enough property to hold a fairly decent position in the world; but with all this I do not want to give myself a name to which others in my place would believe they could lay claim, and I will tell you frankly that I am no gentleman. (Act III, scene XII)*

Le Bourgeois gentilhomme is therefore a more complex literary construction than it appears, using several levels of comedy to arouse laughter in the spectator. In addition to the different types of comedy (gesture, character, situation, words), Molière appropriated a genre that was unpopular at the time – because it was reserved for the people – and gave it unprecedented visibility and success. As usual, he also slipped into his comedy a critique of contemporary society and, in so doing, invited us to re-read his work.

AVENUES FOR REFLECTION

A FEW QUESTIONS FOR FURTHER REFLECTION...

- Why do you think Molière only introduces Mr. Jourdain in the second scene of the play? What is the point of such a late entry?

- What is the real role of the different masters? How do they contribute to the comedy of the play?

- Mrs. Jourdain has a certain conception of marriage; what is it? How does it differ from that of her husband, Mr. Jourdain?

- In what circumstances can it be said that the character of Nicole is an extension of that of Mrs. Jourdain?

- What do you think is the most effective form of comedy in the play? Why or why not?

- Was it necessary for Dorante to know about Cleonte and Covielle's charade? What are their respective interests in this matter?

- Pick out a few expressions that reveal Mr. Jourdain's true social status.

- Characterise the language of the valet, Covielle, by contrasting it with that of the master Cleonte. How do their respective ways of expressing themselves show differing views of love?

- Would removing the dance scenes harm the performance of the play? Consider the pros and cons.

- Watch one of the adaptations of the play (in film or theatre). Compare these different versions. What similarities and differences with the text do you notice?

TO GO FURTHER

REFERENCE EDITION

MOLIÈRE, *Le Bourgeois gentilhomme, Le Médecin malgré lui*, Paris, Maxi-Livres, 2005.

BENCHMARK STUDIES

DANTZIG C., *Dictionnaire égoïste de la littérature française*, Paris, Grasset, 2005.

DE BEAUMARCHAIS J.-P. and COUTY D., *Dictionnaire des grandes œuvres de la littérature française*, Paris, Larousse, 2001.

POLET J.-C. (ed.), *Patrimoine littéraire européen. Avènement de l'équilibre européen (1616-1720)*, tome II, Brussels, De Boeck, 1996.

Your opinion is important to us!
Leave a comment on the website of your online bookshop
and share your favourites on social networks!

www.brightsummaries.com

Ebook EAN: 9782808686471
Paperback EAN: 9782808697873
Legal Deposit: D/2023/12603/1067

Cover: © Primento
Digital conception by Primento, the digital partner of publishers.